THE LAST BELOVED WOMAN

Charles Blake Johnson

AMERICAN TRAIL BOOKS
TOWNSEND

American Trail Books, Inc.
P.O. Box 400
Townsend, Tennessee 37882

Library of Congress Catalog Card Number 93–90882

ISBN 1–884505–00–7

Manufactured in the United States of America

First Edition

FOR ELLEN AND PATTI JUNE

ACKNOWLEDGMENTS

I am deeply indebted to Joe Dan Boyd for his encouragement and firm guidance and to Mary Jane Frederick, whose time, suggestions, friendship and aid have been invaluable over many years.

“Blessed are the peacemakers:
for they shall be called the children of God.”
Matthew 5:9

ONE

Nanye'hi kneeled behind a thick pine tree, trying not to hear the whine of the bullets flying overhead. Her hands worked fast preparing the powder, packing and a ball for Kingfisher's .75–caliber musket. It was a clumsy English-made weapon, weighing eleven pounds, and not very accurate. But it was the best the Cherokees had, and their enemies the Creeks had nothing better.

Kingfisher fired the musket. Nanye'hi heard a loud cry a few yards away. Kingfisher, her husband, made a satisfied grunt, and handed the musket to her to reload. Then he took up his bow, fitted an arrow to it, rose slightly, and shot at yet another Creek across the small clearing before them.

From all around came the sounds of muskets firing. The noise of the musket-balls ripping through the air sounded like a colony of bees on the move. She looked up at Kingfisher and saw a Creek arrow strike the pine tree near his shoulder and bury its point deep in the trunk.

She wished she was home, in Chota, the capital of her people, the Ani-Yun Wiya or Real People. Chota was a place of peace, of refuge and quiet, a restful village on the riverbank where harm came to no one. Her two children were there, and all the good things she had ever known.

But Kingfisher was a warrior and a warrior's place was defending his people. Nanye'hi, niece of the powerful Attakullakulla, the Little Carpenter, belonged with him, even in battle. Women often went with the warriors to battle, helping supply them.

From the beginnings of time, Cherokees and Creeks fought over hunting grounds. Nanye'hi didn't understand it. There was plenty of land for all. But the warriors always wanted more.

Now the Creeks had invaded their land and the Cherokee warriors were fighting back in this battle in the forest at a place called Taliwa. She chewed a bullet to make it more deadly, loaded the mustket, and handed it to Kingfisher.

She saw him stand and then move a bit to get a better shot. Then he grunted again, this time without shooting, and stumbled back, falling to the ground, shot through the chest with a Creek musket ball. His lips were moving, trying to say something.

Nanye'hi stared at him, then heard the brush rattling as someone ran her way. She reached for Kingfisher's musket, turned, and fired just as a Creek warrior leaped for her. The musket-ball found its mark and the man collapsed, his hand holding a knife that just touched Kingfisher's moccasin.

She leaned over Kingfisher, bringing her face to his. "Fight," he said to her. "Fight for the Real People. You must fight or we all die."

"Yes, my husband, I will," she said.

"And then someday, maybe there will be peace for us all," he said. "Live for peace, Wild Rose."

She smiled. As a baby, she was called Tsistima-gis-ke, or Wild Rose. She had known Kingfisher all her life. They ran and played together as children, hunted with their families along the Coosa, the Saluda, the Tugaloo, the Tanasi rivers. He was strong and handsome and some called her beautiful. It was natural that they marry.

And now he was gone. He closed his eyes and she felt the spirit leave his body.

But there was no time for grief. Grieving would come later, in the privacy of her cabin. Now, she must fight.

She reloaded the musket, took up Kingfisher's bow and arrows, along with his knife, and moved among the trees toward the clearing. The other Cherokee warriors saw her and followed.

A Creek man ran into the edge of the clearing, carrying a bow, leading a group of warriors. She stepped into the open and he stopped, staring at the beautiful tall Cherokee woman with long flowing black hair and large shining dark eyes. Quickly, she raised the musket and fired. The Creek fell and the warriors behind him turned back into the trees.

Nanye'hi fired an arrow which struck a Creek warrior before he made it to the forest. Then she ran after the retreating Creeks, shooting two more with arrows. Darting past their bodies, she loaded the musket once more and killed yet another Creek as the war party ran into the distance.

After they disappeared, she fell to her knees gasping. Then the Little Carpenter, brother of her mother Tame Doe, picked her up, grinning. The Carpenter was principal civil chief of the Cherokees. He and Oconostota, the Cherokees' war leader, would have lost much prestige if the Creeks won this battle.

"You saved us!" Little Carpenter said.

"I? I did nothing," Nanye'hi said.

"You did what all the warriors could not do," Oconostota said. "You showed the bravery of the wolf. You are truly of the Wolf Clan."

"I cannot even think of it," she said. "I am a widow now, alone in the world with two children."

"You will never be alone," Little Carpenter said. "You belong to all the Real People. You are the Ghigau!"

"The Ghigau!" Nanye'hi said. "No. Not me. I do not have the strength."

When a woman showed great bravery in war, the Cherokees occasionally gave her the highest honor they gave to women, the Ghigau, or Beloved Woman. This made her a member of the Cherokee council, with a voice equal to that of any man, and the leader of the women's council. It was the most powerful position any Cherokee woman could reach, and no Ghigau had sat with the council for many years.

"You must do it," Little Carpenter said. "Your people need you. This is a hard time and they need the power of the Ghigau. You and you alone are the Beloved Woman. The spirits will speak through you. I've watched you since you were a child, the little Wild Rose, and I've long known you were the one. You cannot deny it. You are the Beloved Woman and you must take your place on the council."

TWO

Riding into Chota after the battle, cries of victory mixed with the wails of the women and children who lost their men in the fight. Tame Doe, Nanye'hi's mother, saw her riding alone and knew Kingfisher was dead. She helped Nanye'hi from the horse and held her head close, pulling her body tight.

Tame Doe knew how it felt to lose a man. Her own husband, Nanye'hi's father, had died many years before, killed during a small fight by a Chickasaw warrior. His name was Francis Ward, and he was a white man, an English soldier sent to Chota to befriend the Cherokees. He had called their only child Nancy, giving her the white name

Nancy Ward. Some of the people of Chota now called her that, too. But to Tame Doe she was always Nanye'hi.

Nanye'hi's father died when she was too young to remember him. But Tame Doe kept his memory alive by teaching the girl English. She was one of the few women in the village who spoke both English and Cherokee. Half-white, half Cherokee, Nanye'hi needed the best of both her worlds to survive. This much Tame Doe knew from the start.

Some of the Ani-Yun Wiya shunned the girl in her early years. "Half this, half that, all of nothing," the cruel children taunted.

But Nanye'hi grew tall and strong and beautiful. She had her father's quickness of mind and her mother's spirit.

Now she returned to Chota a widow, still a young woman. Kingfisher, the warrior seemingly none could defeat, had been killed. Tame Doe remembered when Nanye'hi and Kingfisher were married. The warrior, with a shaved head except for a greased scalplock, brought the bride a deer to show he would always provide for her. Nanye'hi, dressed in a white deer skin decorated with porcupine quills, beads and tassels, gave him an ear of corn to show she would be a good housekeeper.

They had promised to never be separated. But now they were. The ages-old war with the Creeks turned their vows to dust.

Their children would keep the memory alive. The boy, Little Fellow, three years old, came running to Nanye'hi. Her life-long friend, Blossom, came carrying the year-old girl, called Catherine, named after the mother of Nanye'hi's father.

"Your father died a very brave man," she said, collapsing to the ground with her children. "You should be very proud."

The Carpenter walked up then, listening. "But proud, too, of your mother. She is the Ghigau, the

Beloved Woman," he said. "She is the bravest of all."

"The Ghigau!" Tame Doe said.

"She brought us victory," he said. "And now all the people must honor her."

Tame Doe and Blossom looked at Nanye'hi. "Our Nanye'hi, the Ghigau?" Tame Doe said.

"For all time," Little Carpenter said, smiling.

Blossom reached her hand out and touched Nanye'hi's cheek, stroking it. "Little Nancy Ward, the Ghigau," she said.

"I did not ask for this," Nanye'hi said.

"Still, it found you. Wear it well," Blossom said.

In Chota that night, the warriors danced and told the stories of the fight with the Creeks. Nanye'hi, Nancy Ward the half-breed, once called half this, half that, all of nothing, was the heroine of the tales.

The council met and agreed with the Carpenter

that she should be the Ghigau, the Beloved Woman. The Ani-Yun Wiya had long been without a Ghigau. Now, perhaps a Beloved Woman could bring them luck, guidance and leadership.

The Little Carpenter stood before the whole village and told again how Nanye'hi had picked up Kingfisher's weapons and charged the Creeks, killing several and driving them from the field of battle. The people cheered her bravery.

The sound grew loud and lasted long. She looked up into the night sky and saw the sweep of stars Tame Doe said Francis Ward called the Milky Way. The Cherokees said it was formed when brave young men protected an old couple's corn meal from a big dog. The spirit dog flew away into the sky, trailing crumbs of meal that stayed in the sky showing where it went, in honor of the brave young men.

She remembered Kingfisher's dying words, "Live for peace, Wild Rose."

Somewhere in this world of war and death, there must be peace and life, she thought. Somehow, the killing must stop.

She stepped forward to the cheers of her people, led by the Carpenter around a huge bonfire. The yelling was almost as loud as the gunfire in the battle. She smiled, standing straight and tall, moving easily with her uncle. Some children ran out to touch her, and then Little Fellow came and took her hand, walking with her among the people, proud that his mother, among all the women of the Ani-Yun Wiya, was the Beloved Woman.

I accept this, she told herself, only to bring peace. This honor that comes of war will be used for peace.

Then Tame Doe and the Carpenter's wife, Wolf Woman, brought her a white deerskin dress decorated with swan feathers and put it on her. The white swan was the age-old symbol of the Ghigau. Blossom presented her with a swan wing fan and smiled sweetly at her, mouthing the words, "Little Nancy Ward, the Ghigau."

Then Nanye'hi, Nancy Ward the white soldier's daughter, raised her arms high in the air and turned to face her people as their Beloved Woman.

THREE

At dawn the next morning the great war chief Oconostota called for Nanye'hi. She stepped from her cabin into the soft light. The river flowed quietly nearby and to the east the great mountains—The Land of Blue Smoke—pushed skyward in rippling ridges. Her uncle, the Little Carpenter, was there standing silently next to the Real People's head man of war.

In all the years she had known Oconostota, he'd never been to her cabin. "I come to pay homage to the Ghigau," he said.

"I am honored by the presence of a great warrior," she said.

"We must talk," Oconostota said.

She looked to the Carpenter, who smiled his approval. Oconostota set off toward the river, walking easily, not looking back to see if she followed. At the water's edge, he stopped and began to talk.

"You know, of course, how the world was made," he said.

"I have heard it," she said. Since earliest childhood, of course, she had known the tale.

"This land is but an island, floating in the great water, held by a sky-rope at each of the four corners," Oconostota said. "In the beginning, everything was water. The animals in Heaven were very crowded. So the Water-beetle went out across the water and could find no place to stop until it dove to the bottom and came up with mud which it spread until it grew and began this land we call home."

"Yes, I know it," she said.

"The birds came first. The Great Buzzard flew close to the soft earth and where its wings struck ground, valleys were created and mountains pushed up. Then the other animals came and since it was dark, they asked the sun to travel across the sky each day, making light. But the sun was too close to the earth and it was too hot."

"So the witches moved it," she said.

"Yes, the witches moved it, not once but three times until the sun was seven hand-breadths high, at the top of the sky. And the animals and plants tried to keep watch for seven nights, praying. But only the owl, the panther and the wolf could make it through seven nights. So these animals received the power to see at night and prey on those animals that must sleep at night. And of the plants, only the spruce, the pine, the cedar, the laurel and the holly kept awake for all seven nights. So they were allowed to remain green through the winter and provide medicine."

"Then came the Real People," Nanye'hi said.

"A brother and sister at first. And then so many

people, who can count them all? They filled the earth until now how can it hold more? But still the people come."

"Don't forget the end of the story," Nanye'hi said. "Someday the world will become old and wear out. All the people will die. Then the ropes will break, the earth sink into the sea, and all that will be here will be water, as it was in the beginning. Then, perhaps, it all starts over."

Oconostota knelt and put his hand into the cool water. He brought his fingers to his mouth and let a few drops fall on his tongue. "I am afraid, Nancy Ward," he said. "I am afraid the ropes are breaking."

She reached down, putting her hand on the warrior's shoulder. Until yesterday, she would never have dared touch Oconostota. Now, as the Ghigau, she pushed her fear aside, knowing that even the great man of war had the feelings all men had.

"And why is that?" she asked. "Must the ropes break now?"

"Once the Ani-Yun Wiya seemed the center of all things," he said. "The Real People seemed bigger than all the other people put together. Now I see the earth and I hear its tremblings and I wonder what will happen. Sometimes I dream that we are very small. Now the English come asking to build forts on our land to fight their enemies, the French. I don't want to give them the land. Already the whites, the unakas, are coming over The Land of Blue Smoke, building their lodges along the Watauga and the Nolichucky. Where will they go next?"

"Why ask me these things?"

Oconostota sighed and stood, stretching to his full height so that he towered above her. "I come to you because you are the Ghigau," he said. "And because you are half-English, are you not?"

"This doesn't mean I understand them," she said.

"But you speak their language."

"Many of us speak their language."

"What do you think they'll do?" he asked.

"I think no power can stop them from coming across The Land of Blue Smoke," she said. "I think they are so many that the Ani-Yun Wiya means nothing to them."

"Even if we fight?"

"Fighting gains nothing."

Oconostota weighed a small stone in his hand, then skipped it across the water's surface. "I think I will fight, anyway," he said. "I will not give this land away."

"The Ghigau stands for peace," she said. "The land is not ours to give."

"Nancy Ward, as the Ghigau you have the power over our people in peacetime. But I think there will not be very much peace for a long time to come. I think our people will listen to the voice of a warrior."

"And a great warrior you are, Oconostota," she said. "But the day will come when you and I agree that the time for fighting is past."

"What I see is a darkening land," he said, turning back toward the cabin. She walked beside him, hurrying to keep up with his big stride. "Your husband, Kingfisher, was a warrior," he said. "It is up to you to raise your young one as a warrior."

"I stand for peace," she said.

"Kingfisher would want a warrior to take his place," he said, turning for the trail without hesitating.

"Kingfisher called for peace, as well," she said, watching him go. He gave no sign he'd heard, but only kept walking into the woods until he disappeared.

The Carpenter came to her. "He said hard things?" he asked.

"Very hard. He is a troubled man," she said.

"Being the Beloved Woman is not an easy path," he said.

"I didn't ask to be the Ghigau."

"You don't ask for such a thing. It finds you. And if you stand for peace, you are truly the Ghigau, truly our Beloved Woman. Yes, the Ghigau mixes the black drink of war when the warriors set out for a fight. But as the Ghigau, you can make peace between all people. You can put war aside, if enough of us listen. And you can pardon captives of war. Your word is the word of life."

She turned back toward her cabin, seeing Little Fellow standing in the door looking out at her. "Then that is how it will be," she said to Little Carpenter. "As the Ghigau, I will not be happy until all fighting stops."

Watching her walk away, the Carpenter said quietly, "Then your life may be very sad, Wild Rose."

FOUR

The Creeks raided a Cherokee village, killing several warriors and escaping with some women and children, doomed to death or slavery among their enemies. Because of this, the Little Carpenter's son, Dragging Canoe, organized a party of young warriors to move southward punishing the Creeks.

Dragging Canoe was a little younger than his cousin Nanye'hi. He was bigger than an average man, and very strong. His mind was quick and, unlike his father, he lived for war.

He came to Nanye'hi, asking her to mix the black drink of war for his men. "It is your duty," he said.

"I know my duty," she replied. She had already prepared for this, picking the leaves of the winterberry shrub, blending them with other roots and herbs. Now she put the mix in a big clay pot, pouring in water as it sat on the fire in the council house of Chota. The warriors watched as she waved her swan wing over the pot and dropped in leaves from the yaupon shrub. Then each warrior drank, hoping to be purified before battle.

Her brother, Long Fellow, came to her then, settling on the ground beside her, watching. He was already becoming a powerful leader among the people. "It is a good thing you do," he told her. "You should know that I am going to fight our enemies, too."

"I never doubted that you would," she said.

"I will avenge Kingfisher's death," he said.

"If all the Creeks died, it would not avenge Kingfisher," she said, dropping a handful of roots into the kettle.

That night, the warriors drank the black drink and danced until dawn. Then they disappeared on the trail leading to the south. When they returned four days later, they brought captives with them, three young Creek women and a boy of about twelve years. The warriors paraded the captives through Chota and then took them outside the village to an ancient burial mound.

They piled wood on top of the mound and tied the boy on top. The people of Chota stood around the mound, watching as Dragging Canoe spoke of the bravery of his warriors in defeating the Creeks. This captive would show what cowards the Creeks really are, he said.

The boy was shaking and beginning to cry. Dragging Canoe held the thrashing captive with one hand, took his knife and carefully cut the boy's face. Watching the blood pour down, he laughed, stepped back, took a burning torch and lit the wood pile. Smoke poured black and the boy screamed as the fire burned hot around him.

Some of the people from the village turned away, unable to watch the captive's pain and struggle. Then Nanye'hi pushed forward, wearing her white Ghigau dress, carrying a swan wing fan in one hand and a knife in the other. Stepping directly into the flames, she cut the leather straps holding the boy and pulled him from the fire.

"This boy is free!" she yelled.

"No!" Dragging Canoe screamed. "This boy dies for Kingfisher."

"No one dies for Kingfisher," Nanye'hi said. "It is the way he would have wanted it. This boy lives. Let him return to his people and tell them of the brave deeds of the Ani-Yun Wiya. Let him say the Real People are strong enough to free their enemies and have no fear."

The boy stood there looking at her, wiping the blood from his face. She led him to the foot of the mound and gave a little push. "Go," she said. "Go home and never return."

He could not understand her language, though. So she pointed at the forest to the south and shoved him again. This time he ran hard for the trees, and soon was gone from sight.

Long Fellow stepped to Nanye'hi's side and put his arms around her. "You are truly the Ghigau," he said. "Even Dragging Canoe believes it is so."

The people of Chota cleared a pathway for her as she walked back to her cabin. They were silent, watching her, even the Carpenter and Tame Doe and Blossom. When she got to the cabin, she slumped on the floor by the doorway, put her face in her hands, and began to cry.

Little Fellow pulled away from his grandmother, Tame Doe, and ran inside to be with her. He put his hand on her shoulder as she cried and said, "Don't worry, all the bad is gone."

Touching his face, she sat him in her lap. "I'm

afraid the bad is just beginning, little one," she said.

She thought about the new English forts even then being built in the Cherokee country. There were three of them and one was near Chota, at the junction of the Tellico River with the Little Tanasi River that flowed by the village. It frightened her to have 200 English soldiers so near, with Cherokee warriors bound by a treaty to fight for them against the French.

The Carpenter said the Cherokees needed the English provisions for the unending wars against the Creeks and the Chickasaws, who lived further west near the Great River. With the English guns in hand, 100 Cherokees had gone north with the English to fight the Shawano Indians who sided with the French in this white man's war. They found the English did not know how to fight in the woods, starving them, until they turned southward for home.

On the way home, white settlers attacked the

Cherokees, killing 40 of them. Dragging Canoe and his warriors wanted to kill these whites. But the Carpenter and even Oconostota were against it until the English at Fort Prince George built near the Cherokee town of Keowee at the headwaters of the Savannah River attacked the village while the men were away hunting and killed many women and children. Nothing could hold back the warriors then and they rode against the Carolina settlements and even attacked Fort Loudon near Chota.

The Carpenter couldn't understand why the English feared the Cherokees. Many years before, he'd been sent with six other Cherokee leaders across the great sea to England. In the king's palace, Whitehall, they signed a treaty paper and gave gifts to the king. When they returned home, Little Carpenter had been certain the king loved the Cherokees and would not break the promises of the treaty. Now, he wondered if he had been wrong.

If the Carpenter could not understand it, how could she? Nanye'hi hugged her son and rocked back and forth, still crying. What would become of the Ani-Yun Wiya? She recalled the tales of the smallpox sickness that struck the people when she was a small child, killing half of them. Some of the ones who survived were so horrified by the terrible scars the disease left that they took their own lives.

That had been a white man's disease, something the people had never seen before. Now, with the white people pushing all around them, she wondered what would happen. Would there be more disease, more war, more death?

Surely something terrible blew on the wind. She kissed the top of Little Fellow's head, wishing that he could live in peace and safety. She thought about the frightened Creek boy she had sent running for home, and smiled.

"I am the Ghigau," she said to herself.

FIVE

Before long, fights between the Cherokees and the English were a common thing. The warriors left the villages to raid the forts nearby, returning each time with dead and wounded. They asked the Ghigau's blessing, and for her to mix the black drink. She did, though it became harder and harder as she saw the sadness of death on her people.

Oconostota and 31 other leaders went to Fort Prince George to talk peace. But the governor seized them there, forcing them into a small room, holding them as prisoners. Then he sent 1,400 soldiers to fight the Cherokees on their own ground.

The Little Carpenter, hating the war, remembering the good things he knew to be true about the

English, went to the fort with Dragging Canoe and asked for Oconostota's release. The English let the war chief and three others go after they signed a paper agreeing to fight for the English against the French.

On the way to Chota, Dragging Canoe was furious at Oconostota for signing the agreement. "It is only paper," Oconostota said. "Paper means nothing. Scratches on paper, what is that? It tells nothing of my heart."

"You did what they asked," Dragging Canoe said.

"From this day forward, no white man is my friend," Oconostota said. "Now, I fight until I can fight no longer."

The Carpenter stopped them. "I've been among the English and learned that fighting them is no good. They outnumber the ants that live on the ground. Kill a thousand and ten thousand will replace them. Kill ten thousand and ten times ten thousand will come in their footsteps. Nothing will be accomplished but to hurt our own people," he said.

"They put the fear into your heart," Dragging Canoe said.

"A little fear is better than blind and foolish courage," Little Carpenter said, walking on.

Oconostota and Dragging Canoe looked at each other. Oconostota shook his head, pitying the older man. Dragging Canoe followed his father and Oconostota walked slightly apart until they came to the outskirts of Chota.

Once there, an uneasy stillness overwhelmed them. They heard children crying and dogs barking, but no one moved about the village. Nanye'hi ran toward them, then stopped a distance away.

"You must leave," she said. "It is not safe in Chota."

"Creeks or English? Who does this?" Oconostota asked.

"No, it is the smallpox," she said. "Go away while you can."

"I am a strong man," Dragging Canoe said. "Smallpox cannot harm me."

"A strong man is nothing to the smallpox," she said.

"I have a wife and child here. I will enter," he said.

Oconostota and the Carpenter stood together watching him walk past Nanye'hi into the midst of Chota and turn for his cabin. The Carpenter looked at Oconostota. "A little fear?" he asked, shaking his head. Then he went up the trail, walking in the fading light.

Oconostota watched him go and then turned back to Nanye'hi. "You are well, Nancy Ward?" he asked.

"Yes," she said. "I think my white blood protects me."

He looked at her sadly and finally followed Little Carpenter away from the village.

She went back to her house and tended Tame Doe, who had the sickness. Tame Doe was very hot, fevered, and her skin had the blotches the disease left. Little Fellow and his sister Catherine had gone with Blossom to her cabin to get away from the sickness. There was talk of taking them far away, deep into the forest to escape it.

Some said witches brought the disease. Others believed it was the Little People, the woods fairies. Nanye'hi knew it came from the white man, a weapon more deadly than anything that could be used to destroy the Ani-Yun Wiya.

It comes from the white man's breath, she told herself. It comes from deep within him.

She lay down next to Tame Doe, holding the older woman's hand. In the middle of the night, Tame Doe woke, sweating, the fever breaking.

Nanye'hi hugged her close when she began to chill and shake. By morning, it seemed Tame Doe would live.

After a few hours and drinking some hot broth, Tame Doe sat up and began to talk. "You are the Ghigau but I am still your mother," she said. "There are things you should know before I die."

"But you are getting well," Nanye'hi said.

"The day comes when we all will die and we never know when that will be. It could be today or tomorrow. Who knows?"

"Do not talk of it," Nanye'hi said.

"Now is the time for talk, now, when the sickness is still upon us. Some people say the sickness comes of evil magic. But we know that cannot be. What have we done wrong that we should be punished so? Others say it comes from the English, and this thing I believe. We never had it before the English crossed The Land of Blue Smoke," Tame

Doe said, sipping her broth, leaning back against the cabin wall.

"Even so, that does not make the English bad. I believe this is a thing beyond their power to stop. It is a part of them, yet not a part of them. Your father was English and he was a good man. He came from across the great water to this very place and found me. Me! Of all the women of our people, he chose me. And I believe it was because of my dream. I had dreamed of a tall pale man who traveled a great distance to get to me. He had the power of the wolf and the laughter of the otter deep within him. There was nothing bad inside your father. He served his king but he brought the Real People many good things."

Tame Doe moved forward and pulled Nanye'hi's hair back behind her head, braiding it. "So never believe those people who say all the English are evil or that all the English do this or that. And these people coming to live in our country, remember that they are people just as we are. Your father prophesied they would come here from across the mountains and someday build great towns like those across the sea. We cannot stop them. We must learn to live with them," she said.

"These things have been in my thoughts, also," Nanye'hi said. "If the whites are bad, well, I am half-white, so what does that make me? I do not think I am evil. And I know that fighting the whites will come to no good."

Tame Doe sat back, looking at Nanye'hi, putting a hand softly on her daughter's cheek. "I had another dream in my sickness," she said. "I dreamed that a white man came for you, a white man like your father."

"Mother, this cannot be. I am Kingfisher's wife forever."

"As you should be. But you can take another man for a husband. You are a young woman. You need a man. And I want more grandchildren."

"But a white man! This could be only trouble, mother."

"It was in my dream," Tame Doe said. "I cannot say why."

This troubled Nanye'hi very much. She rose and stood in the cabin doorway looking out across the village at the river. She saw Dragging Canoe's wife, Leaf, walking by the water. She was crying and cutting her hair with a trade knife.

Nanye'hi went to her. "What is wrong, sister?" she asked.

"My child is dead," Leaf said. "The white man's disease killed him. And this morning, Dragging Canoe has the fever. If he dies, too, I will have no reason to live."

Taking the sobbing woman in her arms, hugging her tight in sorrow, Nanye'hi felt hot tears on her shoulder. Then she began to cry, too, thinking of the dead child and of Dragging Canoe and of the hardships coming for the Real People.

SIX

By the cold winter months of the year the whites called 1760, Dragging Canoe recovered from his sickness. Oconostota traveled among the villages talking of war against the whites. In council, the Little Carpenter spoke of his friendship for the English people, of how war could come to no good. Nanye'hi, the Ghigau, said only peace could make the Ani-Yun Wiya happy.

"We live now with death all around us," she said. "Let us not invite it in the door of our houses."

She stood, tall and lean and beautiful, outlined against the log fire of the council house. "Remember the mother bear's song," she said. "Remember the mother bear and what she said to her young."

Then Nanye'hi began to sing. She sang:

"If you hear the noise of the chase
Going down the stream
Then run up the stream.
If you hear the noise of the chase
Going up the stream
Then run to the high mountain,
Then run to the high mountain."

She looked around her at the silent faces lit by the firelight, then sat down. "That is all the words I have," she said.

After a long silence, Oconostota stood and looked at her. Then, without a word, he walked out the door. Dragging Canoe, the smallpox scars still fresh on his face, moved to his father the Little Carpenter and touched his shoulder. Then he followed Oconostota into the darkness of the forest.

Within a few days Oconostota and Dragging

Canoe gathered the young men and went to Fort Prince George, where the chiefs taken prisoner with Oconostota were still kept in the log jailhouse building. They surrounded the fort so no one could go in or out. After many days of siege passed, Oconostota sent a woman to the fort to ask the commander to come outside to talk. As soon as he was clear of the fort, Oconostota waved a bridle over his head as a signal to the other warriors, and they shot the officer.

When the soldiers inside the fort saw this, they went into the room where the Cherokee chiefs were held prisoner and killed them all.

Then Oconostota led the warriors in raids against the frontier settlements. Back at Fort Loudon, near Chota, the Ani-Yun Wiya surrounded the stockade, refusing to allow anyone to pass through their lines.

Nanye'hi walked among the warriors, bringing food so they might remain strong. "War is a very bad thing," she told Tame Doe, who went with her. "But it would be even worse to abandon our own men."

An army of 1,600 white soldiers began moving down the river toward Chota, killing any Indians they found. In a council at Chota, the men decided to meet the white army and fight before they reached the village. Nanye'hi did not speak against this. She did not speak at all in this council. She went outside and mixed the black drink of war for the warriors. Then she sat against the wall of her cabin, looking at the bright sweep of the stars overhead.

Why do men fight? Why do men kill? She thought about it for a very long time and decided nothing. Why?

The warriors drove off the army of white men, killing and wounding nearly one hundred of them. But many warriors were also killed and hurt. Dragging Canoe came home with a wounded arm.

Nanye'hi mixed herbs with mud and put some on the wound so it would heal quickly.

The siege of Fort Loudon went on for two months. With the white army defeated, no one could save the soldiers inside. Captain Demere, the commander, sent a message out one day asking to speak with Nanye'hi.

She went inside the fort and was shocked to see the pale and sick people inside. There were women and small children who looked as though they were dying of starvation. The soldiers were thin and their clothing hung loosely off their bodies. It was painful to look in their eyes. She almost felt ashamed for being well-fed and healthy.

Captain Demere said, "Nancy Ward, you are a good woman, and you have influence over your people. You can see that we are starving. Can you help us?"

"The warriors will allow no food to pass to the

fort," she said. "You should give up the fort. Ask for mercy. We are not an evil people. Leave our country and we will let you go."

In a few days, Captain Demere surrendered to Oconostota. He promised to give up all their weapons except for guns and ammunition to hunt as they left the Cherokee country. They would never return to Fort Loudon, he said.

Oconostota let the 200 English soldiers, with their few women and children, safely leave the fort and camp for the night several miles away. The warriors looked around in the fort and then found bags of ammunition and gunpowder buried inside. Weapons, cannons and amunition had been dumped into the river alongside the fort to keep the warriors from using them.

This deceit enraged Oconostota. At dawn the next morning, he led the warriors against the English camp, killing Captain Demere and 29 of his soldiers. The warriors took the rest of the soldiers prisoners of war, holding them for the high ransom the English would pay to get them back.

The Carpenter found an Englishman he liked, Captain Stuart, and saved him from either a life of slavery or being tortured and killed. Claiming Stuart as his own prisoner, the Carpenter spent nine days taking him to safety in Virginia.

Nanye'hi was saddened by what happened to the English soldiers. She nursed the wounded back to health and kept one white woman and a young child in her own house, protecting them from the wild forest and the warriors' raging fury.

The white woman had been surprised by her kindness, and her use of the English language. When word came that the woman had been ransomed by the English, at first she didn't want to go. She was afraid of the violence and hatred of the wilderness war.

"You must go home and tell the whites that all

of us here are not bad people," Nanye'hi said. "We have kindness in our hearts and a great country that belongs to no person but is a part of every one of us. The same house shelters us and the same sky covers us all. Tell them Nancy Ward says it is so."

SEVEN

Now the battles came one after the other. The English were helped by the Chickasaws, the Ani-Yun Wiya's old enemy to the west. Their army pushed through the valleys, destroying villages, burning crops and orchards. With the warriors dying of their wounds, the women's cries filled the long nights.

Those whose villages were burned by the English ran toward the mountains, higher and higher, hiding in caves, eating roots and wild things they would never have touched in their old lives. In a year of fighting, the Ani-Yun Wiya lost half their warriors.

The Little Carpenter went to Charleston in September, 1761, making a peace treaty to end the war. Nanye'hi understood from the beginning that the Real People could never win this fight. No one wins a war, she thought. Every war is lost. Whenever the warriors came back shouting with a victory, waving white men's scalps as they danced around the fire, she knew that in the end they would lose. No matter how many times they won, it would all end with losing.

With the new peace, however, things quieted. The Cherokees went back to their homes, rebuilt their cabins, replanted their fields, and learned again to laugh. Nanye'hi taught her son to ride horseback, and she and Tame Doe worked with her daughter Catherine until the little girl could sew her own dresses.

White traders came to the villages again, trading cloth and gunpowder and food for whatever things of value the Cherokees might offer. One day Nanye'hi was out walking in the forest when a tall white man rode up. He was mounted on a large roan-colored horse, leading three mules with heavy packs of goods. He began speaking broken Cherokee, making no sense. Nanye'hi laughed, and he stopped, looking foolish.

"We may speak English together," she said.

"An English-speaking woman?" he said. "Wonders never cease out here in the backwoods. Allow me to introduce myself, then, ma'am. My name is Brian Ward."

Her breath caught in her throat. She raised a hand and started to speak but couldn't.

"Ma'am? Are you all right?" he asked.

"I am fine," she said finally. "I was just a little surprised. My own father's name was Ward."

"Is that right? I'm told an uncle of mine did a little trading out this way a long time back. He never came home. We always wondered what happened."

"He died here. It was many years ago. I cannot

even remember him. But my mother says he was a great man," she said.

"Well, by Joseph, that would make us cousins of a sort, wouldn't it? And what do you call yourself, ma'am?"

"Nanye'hi is my name."

He struggled to say it, trying so hard that she began to laugh again. "But the white people call me Nancy," she said. "Nancy Ward. That will do."

She led him back to Chota. Right away he was busy trading the goods he'd brought on the mules for the animal skins the people had been saving for a trade day. He was friendly, joking in English with the men who understood the language. People liked him, and his trades were fair.

That night he came to her cabin and offered a hunk of venison from a deer he'd shot along the trail. She roasted it over the fire. Waiting to eat, he entertained Tame Doe with tales of the white settlements, then he played stick games with Little

Fellow and pulled a real doll from a pack for Catherine. The little girl laughed and held it like a baby, rocking it back and forth, talking to it as though it was real. Soon she began playing her own games with it.

After dinner that night, he moved back to the camp he had made at the edge of Chota. Tame Doe stood watching him go, then said to Nanye'hi, "Remember my dream, daughter. Remember my dream of the white man."

"I remember," she said. "But dreams are not real."

"This man is real," Tame Doe said. "I think he has come for you. What else can it be?"

"But, mother, a white man? Why a white man? I just don't think that was meant to be."

"You are half white yourself. If you reject the white man, you reject yourself."

"I don't know. I have more to think of than just myself. Now I am the Ghigau. Can the Beloved

Woman take a white man for her husband? The Ghigau belongs to all."

"But first you belong to yourself. Follow your heart," Tame Doe said, turning for her cabin.

Nanye'hi knew that many women of her people married white men. Her own mother had done so. But too often the marriage came to nothing. The men left, going home to the towns across the mountains, never returning. Or the men were killed fighting the Cherokees when times turned hard. She thought of the women who had loved the soldiers of Fort Loudon before the siege. After the siege and the battle, when the Englishmen were either killed or taken prisoner, the women had been very sad, knowing they would never see their men again.

Love is a hard enough thing, she thought, without the difference of skin color turning man and woman against each other.

No man could replace Kingfisher. Yet she had

gone several years with no man to share her life. The women of Chota were always coming up with one man or another they thought would make her a good husband. But she never paid much attention. And now, with so many warriors killed in the war against the English, there weren't many men available for marriage.

The white trader came to her cabin each day for the next two weeks, sharing food and telling tales of the white world far beyond the mountains, and even in Ireland, his native home. The children sat awestruck as he told of the vast cities of Charleston and Savannah, with huge homes made of brick and thousands of people walking cobblestone streets.

"He is a manly man," Blossom said to Nanye'hi one day after he'd gone back to his trading.

"Then take him for your own," Nanye'hi said.

Blossom's husband had been killed in the fighting against the whites. Realizing the cruelty of her words, Nanye'hi put her hand on her friend's arm and shook her head.

"Excuse me. All this is very confusing," Nanye'hi said. "Everyone in Chota talks about the attention he gives me, and I don't even want it. I am not acting myself."

"He's in love. It is easy to see. And you need a man," Leaf said.

Nanye'hi laughed and walked to her corn field. She pulled the grass from the clay soil and tried not to think of anything else.

But she had grown used to Brian Ward's visits and his easy way of talking. The next morning, Brian Ward didn't come to her cabin. She waited, then walked to his camp. But he was already gone.

No matter, she told herself. Tame Doe was an old woman with an old woman's dreams, and Blossom still behaved like a silly child. Nanye'hi had been married once, and once was enough. She had her two children, and her place with her people. Moving among them, speaking quietly to the women who even now were beginning to sew dresses made from the cloth the trader had brought, Nanye'hi put Brian Ward out of her mind.

She had more important things to do than worry about a man. Back at her cabin, Catherine was crying. She had a bad dream, she said, and now she felt sick, coughing and feverish.

Nanye'hi knew just what to do. She quickly mixed some liverwort into a hot tea. The girl drank it and right away looked better, smiling sweetly as she relaxed on her bed.

Being a mother is enough, Nanye'hi told herself, looking at her daughter. Who needs a man?

EIGHT

By the time the leaves turned gold and yellow and brown on the high slopes of the Land of Blue Smoke, Brian Ward had come back to Chota. He built a little cabin to house his trade goods and set up shop, waiting for the Real People to come to him.

He spent his spare time with Nanye'hi. She grew used to him being there, and learned to do her work even as he told his stories. Tame Doe and Blossom and the other women liked to listen to him talk of the white settlements and the wondrous things he had seen during his travels.

One day he brought a deer carcass to her, dressed for cooking, leaving it hanging by the door. She had been telling Catharine the story about why the turkey gobbles. But now she looked up, seeing Brian standing in the doorway.

"Isn't that how they do it?" he asked.

"Do what?"

"When a warrior asks a woman to be his wife, he brings her a deer, does he not?"

"That is what some men do," she said. "But I am not looking for a husband. I need nothing. I have everything I want."

"That's why I want you," he said, stepping up to touch her forehead with a big hand. "You don't need me, but I need you."

She turned away but then he pulled her to him. Putting her head on his shoulder, she thought of Kingfisher and Tame Doe's dream and her own two children. "I will be your woman," she said softly.

Their wedding was a glorious thing. Nanye'hi wore her Ghigau costume. Tame Doe made Brian a pair of soft new buckskin trousers, with a shirt to match. Everyone in Chota came to the ceremony, and many friends from other villages visited, too. Oconostota and the Little Carpenter were there, looking on proudly. Dragging Canoe, however, stayed back at the edge of the crowd. "Nothing good will come of this," he had told Nanye'hi, and he meant it.

Despite her cousin's prophesy, Brian Ward made her happy. True, he left often to return to the white settlements east of the mountains, or to trade with other Cherokee villages. But he stayed with Nanye'hi for long periods. It felt good to have a man again, she decided, and within a year, she had another daughter. She named the girl Elizabeth, after her Brian's mother.

White settlers began building homes on the western side of the mountains, along the Watauga and Holston rivers, far beyond the boundary set for them by the English treaties. Dragging Canoe,

Oconostota and their friend, The Raven, a Shawnee who had married a Cherokee woman and was now an important man in Chota, wanted to drive out the settlers. Nanye'hi's brother, Long Fellow, now the head man of seven villages, voted to wait before spilling more blood, joining the Carpenter and Nanye'hi in calling for peace.

The Ani-Yun Wiya admired some of the new settlers for the hard work put into building a home in the wild country. Some were great hunters, like Daniel Boone, liked by many Cherokees even though he broke the treaty laws in traveling their country.

Brian Ward wandered freely among the people, trading goods. Sometimes Nanye'hi went with him, visiting friends and relatives in the villages. It was a good time, a time of happiness, a time when even Nanye'hi could put the white settlements out of her mind.

Finally, though, Brian went east to the towns

across the mountains, and never returned. She waited a long time, hoping to see him again. But he did not come home to Chota.

Seeing her sadness, Dragging Canoe and The Raven and two other men of Chota rode to see what happened to the trader. They were gone a month. Then Dragging Canoe came to her cabin while the others returned to their own homes.

She offered him a pipe of tobacco and some roasted wild turkey Little Fellow had shot that morning. He sat back, tired from the long ride, his pock-marked face looking grim.

"It is a hard thing I have to say," he said. "But I saw it with my own eyes and I know it to be true. You share Brian Ward with a white woman. They have a home far away over the mountains, and three children. He would leave you here, then go there and stay with her. We went to the house. The woman was scared and began screaming, so he came to the door with his rifle and told us to leave.

I wanted to kill him then, but thought I would ask you first. Do you want him killed?"

"No killing. Not for me. It is not worth it," she said, tears coming to her eyes.

"But you are no ordinary woman," Dragging Canoe said. "You are the Ghigau. He treats you with disrespect. No one disrepects the Ghigau. Not without paying for it."

"Leave him unharmed," she said. "Let no blood flow over this thing. If you kill him, there could be another war."

Dragging Canoe put the pipe aside, sitting up straight, looking outside the cabin. "Make no mistake, there will be another war. The whites want it. They want to drive us from this country. They want to kill us all," he said. "They cannot be trusted. Look at Brian Ward. He smiles, he laughs, he trades, he gives you a child. Then he leaves and goes back to his white world. All this means nothing to him. He takes, he uses, then he throws it away as though it is dirt."

After Dragging Canoe left for the night, Nanye'hi lay in bed, holding Elizabeth in her arms. After the child went to sleep she thought of Brian Ward. Perhaps he did run away. Perhaps he had a reason. He could have feared the hot-blooded warriors like Dragging Canoe. Or he could have had another reason, something to do with her. Maybe she drove him away, but she couldn't think of anything she had done.

She closed her eyes but could not sleep. The tears came throughout the long night.

NINE

Come morning, she resolved never to cry another tear for a man. Brian Ward had no place in her life, and she would live for the Ani-Yun Wiya, the Real People, her people. She went to the river and bathed, washing her hair. When she dried off on the bank, she felt fresh, renewed, alive again.

With each passing day, more white settlers came into the Cherokee country. On March 17, 1775, at a place along the Watauga River called Sycamore Shoals, the Cherokee chiefs sold the whites their lush lands that lay between the Kentucky and Cumberland rivers. Never again would the rich Kentucky hunting grounds be theirs.

At the Sycamore Shoals treaty council, Oconostota spoke against giving away their lands. Nanye'hi thought the Brave Warrior of the Cherokees was now an old man. He had been wounded several times, and caught the white man's sicknesses, so that his body was now frail. But he spoke like a young man, asking his kinsmen to not give up their lands.

In the midst of the treaty-making, Dragging Canoe leaped into the circle of speakers, shouting against signing the white man's paper. Looking the whites directly in the eye, pointing toward the west where the land being sold was located, he yelled, "There is a dark cloud hanging over that country. It is a dark and bloody ground. You will pay a heavy price if you take it from us."

Nanye'hi found it difficult to watch. She rose and stood at the edge of the forest, looking up at the mountains nearby. Her people had given up 20 million acres of land for trade goods worth ten thousand English pounds sterling. These numbers meant nothing to her. All she knew was that the world was closing down around her and her people. Someday the white man would know what the Real People had always known: that they could no more own the land than they could the wolf that walked upon it.

But she knew when the whites learned this, it would be too late. The Ani-Yun Wiya would be gone, as the buffalo had already left this land.

She was still standing there when Blossom walked up to her with Little Fellow and Catherine following. "Now we will have some nice things. Money, even," Blossom said.

"Money is nothing," Nanye'hi told her. "Less than nothing. What things can we use when our lives are gone?"

Before long, the settlers calling themselves Americans were fighting the English soldiers. The Little Carpenter explained that the Americans wanted to be free from the rule of the English king.

That was not so easy enough to understand. But in the summer of 1775, the English soldiers supplied the Cherokees with weapons and ammunition to fight the Americans.

Cherokees led by Dragging Canoe and Tories, English sympathizers dressed like Cherokees, raided American settlements on the eastern slopes of the mountains. Englishmen worked among the villages, bringing with them almost anything the people needed, talking about the war with the Americans.

Nanye'hi spoke against the war. Why should brothers who spoke the same langauge have to fight each other? It was easier to understand the old fight between the French and the English. This war was a very bad thing. She said the Ani-Yun Wiya should not take sides but sit back and see what happened.

Dragging Canoe's warriors wanted the guns the Englishmen offered. They would help fight against the Chickasaws and Creeks, the old enemies who still from time to time raided the villages. The Americans were hungry for land, taking what did not belong to them, killing the game so that now a man could walk all day without sighting a deer.

In May, 1776, a Shawnee chief, Cornstalk, arrived in Chota. He was a big man, full of talk and anger. He had 14 chiefs of northern tribes with him. They came from the Iroquois, Mohawks, Shawnees, Ottawas, Delawares, and Nantucas.

Cornstalk asked all the Cherokee leaders to meet with him in ten days. He said that all the Indian tribes should work together with the English against the American settlers. He spoke of all the whites he saw on his 70-day trip from his country to the Land of Blue Smoke. Let the English soldiers attack from the great sea to the east and the red men push hard from the west and the settlers would surely be defeated, Cornstalk said.

Nanye'hi tried to speak to Cornstalk. She

wanted to tell him that war would accomplish nothing, that only peace could help their people. But he knew nothing of the Cherokee's Ghigau and would not speak with her. To him, she was just a woman.

And Cornstalk thought the Little Carpenter, who spoke for peace, was just a tired old man getting in the way.

But Cornstalk's words enflamed Dragging Canoe and his young warriors. Even before the ten days of talk ended, they were preparing for war, sharpening knives, repairing guns, making new moccasins. One night Dragging Canoe and some others slipped away from the village. They returned a few days later with four white scalps, proudly presented as a gift to Cornstalk.

The Raven and Dragging Canoe exchanged war belts with the Shawnees and Ottawas and Mohawks. This meant that they agreed to fight as brothers with each other against the American settlers. During the council, Cornstalk brought out a war belt nine feet long, colored purple, that made the others in the council house gasp in admiration. Then he poured vermillion, a red paint, over it, symbolizing blood, the blood that now bound them, and the blood they would spill.

Nearly all the Indians roared their approval. Dragging Canoe stepped forward to receive the belt, his eyes wide with excitement. The young men began to dance wildly, whirling, jumping, shouting with the thought of victory.

Nanye'hi sat silently, watching all this. She looked at the Carpenter and Oconostota, who sat quietly together, not moving, looking worried. She went to them and put her hand on the Carpenter's arm.

"Uncle, this is a hard time," she said.

"I can only remember the last time we took the warpath against the whites," he said. "Half our young men died."

"This Cornstalk is a brave man but foolish," Oconostota said. "I am old. I can no longer fight such a man."

That night, Dragging Canoe and his men took prisoner three white traders doing business at Chota. He suspected them of spying on the Cherokee villages for the Watauga settlers. After locking them in a cabin, Dragging Canoe and his 700 warriors made plans to attack the settlers.

Nanye'hi mixed the black drink for the war preparations, as the Ghigau must. The large war kettle was brought outside from the council fire of the Town House, placed over another fire, and filled with water. Wearing her white dress decorated with swan fans, she carried a deerskin bag, sprinkling the herbal mix around Oconostota and Dragging Canoe.

With a strong sweep of her arm, she threw the rest of the herbs in the fire. Then she chanted the song of Nunyunuwi, the Stone Man, the people-eating monster covered with stone who lived in the mountains. Only the power of women could defeat the Stone Man, and when he died in the fire of the medicine-man, he gave up his secrets to the Ani-Yun Wiya.

After the song, she dropped a branch of the yaupon shrub into the kettle. When the water simmered, mixing all the herbs within, the drink would be ready.

Sitting down after she finished, she watched the warriors, flushed with excitement, shouting, dancing, firing rifles into the air. They were eager for the hunt, ready for blood, to kill or be killed. She knew they could not be stopped.

Soon, no one paid attention to her. She went to the cabin holding the white traders. One was her good friend, Isaac Thomas, a fair and truthful man. The others were William Fallin and Jarret Williams, both married to women of the Ani-Yun Wiya.

She untied the rope holding the cabin door closed. "You must go," she said to Isaac.

"Oh, by Joseph, I knew we were good as dead," he said. "Thank you, Nancy, thank you. You're God's own angel."

"Go quickly," she said. "Go to the settlements and tell them 700 warriors will attack. They will divide and some go with The Raven against the Carter's Valley settlements. More will go with Dragging Canoe to the Great Island of the Holston. Abram, the man from Chilhowee town, takes the rest against the Americans at Watauga. Then they'll meet and raid up into Virginia. Go now or all will be lost, including your lives."

Isaac stepped to her and kissed her lightly on the cheek. "I'd marry you, Nancy Ward, if you'd give me half a chance," he said, laughing.

"Don't tempt me," she said. "Now be on your way, and hurry."

The men faded into the forest, running quickly

through the darkness. She watched them go, then turned for her own cabin. The children were huddled by the doorway, except for Little Fellow, now a young man calling himself Five Killer, who was dancing with Dragging Canoe.

"Get to sleep," she said.

Seeing her dark mood, the girls went to bed and lay quietly under the covers. She sat by the door, listening to the wild shouts coming from the dance.

Have all the earth's people gone crazy? she asked herself.

TEN

The men came back from the war trail angry and disappointed. Dragging Canoe had terrible wounds in both thighs. Carried home by his warriors, Nanye'hi saw him lying in pain at Big Island Town where he now lived. He spat his disgust at her.

"They were waiting for us!" he said. "Somebody warned them. They were in their forts, and then when we came upon the Great Island, they ambushed us. They fought as we do, hiding behind trees and rocks, not in the open like the English. Right there, thirteen warriors fell dead and we had to leave them behind."

To keep their honor, Dragging Canoe's men attacked solitary cabins on the outskirts of the settlements, killing 18 whites. The Raven had found nothing but deserted cabins at Carter's Valley. Abram did no better at Watauga, with a siege of the fort accomplishing nothing.

But Abram did return with two prisoners and a few cows, taking them to his town of Chilhowee. One prisoner was a woman, Lydia Bean. She had been captured trying to drive her cows into the safety of the fort. A boy taken with her, Samuel Moore, was burned at the stake soon after Abram's party reached home.

Nanye'hi heard about the woman. Lydia Bean had already been condemned to die by Abram and the other warriors, who were furious over the failure of their strike against the settlers.

"There is nothing to be done for her. It is better to remain silent," the Little Carpenter said.

Dragging Canoe, his wounded legs in great pain, laughed when he heard about the prisoner. "I wish I could be there to light the fire under her," he said, and Nanye'hi soon heard about his harsh judgement.

Nanye'hi saddled a horse and rode for Chilhowee, though. The Bean woman must be saved, she told herself, hoping she could get there before the execution.

When she rode into Chilhowee, Mrs. Bean was already tied to a wood frame on top of the mound outside the village. Flames were beginning to leap from a pile of wood at the prisoner's feet. The woman began to shriek and scream as Nanye'hi pushed the horse hard toward where the people gathered around the mound.

She jumped off the horse and ran up the mound. In her Ghigau costume, she stepped directly into the fire. With a sharp knife she cut the ropes binding the woman and pulled her away from the flames, kicking at the burning wood at her feet. She held Mrs. Bean up in front of her and faced the crowd.

"Look at what you do!" Nanye'hi said. "Brave warriors torturing women! It revolts my soul. Look in her face. Do you see the face of an enemy to be feared? This woman's death would bring us no good. I free this woman. She will go home with me."

The people of Chilhowee, silent as a lizard crawling upon a rock, stood aside as she brought the Bean woman down from the mound and put her on her horse. Pulling herself up behind her, Nanye'hi said, "Send me her cows."

Abram stepped up, shaking his head. "There are a few left but we plan to eat them. They are not so good as a deer but our hunting has been poor."

"Have them sent to me," she said.

"You demand many things," he said.

"I demand nothing but what is right."

As she trotted the horse through Chilhowee and onto the trail to Chota, she felt the Bean woman collapse against her. Softly, as she would hold a child, she kept the prisoner upright and safe on the horse.

Back in Chota, Mrs. Bean pulled away from Nanye'hi, crawling to a corner of the cabin.

"You have nothing to fear from me," Nanye'hi said.

"You speak English!" the woman said, surprised.

"Yes, my father was English."

"What are you going to do with me? Make me a slave? If you do, I'll kill myself first."

"Mrs. Bean, I plan to keep you here until you can be safely returned to your home. I am sorry for the way my people have treated you. They are very angry just now."

"I'll say they're angry. They burned that Moore boy on the fire like animals. Animals! They were laughing about it. And then they tried to do it to me. What did I ever do to them? It was awful. Just horrible."

The white woman began to cry, putting her face in her hands. Finally, she stretched out full upon the ground and sobbed while Nanye'hi watched. After several minutes, she sat up, wiping her face with her hands, looking at Nanye'hi.

"What's your name, anyway?" she said. "Somebody saves you, you ought to know their name."

"My name is Nanye'hi. But the whites call me Nancy Ward."

"I've heard of you. They say you're somebody special, that you have a power over these Indians."

"Not enough, unfortunately, as you can see."

"I owe you something for saving me. I'll repay you somehow one of these days," Mrs. Bean said.

"There is a way to repay me now," Nanye'hi said. "Soon your cows will be here. I want you to teach me the secret of milk."

"Secret of milk?"

"Yes. Teach me how you make things from it."

"You mean butter? And cheese?"

"Yes. I think it would be good for my people to know these things."

So the next day, Mrs. Bean began showing Nanye'hi how to care for cows and milk them. As the days passed, she made butter and then cheese, teaching Nanye'hi how to do it.

As soon as Dragging Canoe could walk without terrible pain, he and his warriors began raiding the settlements. Nanye'hi could not stop them, but she refused to give her blessing. Knowing Mrs. Bean was teaching Nanye'hi about cattle and milk, the warriors brought her many captured cattle taken in raids.

Her cattle herd grew. She and Mrs. Bean began to show the other women about the good things that come from milk.

The whites could not take Dragging Canoe's strikes against them for long without fighting back. By September 1776, 5,000 American soldiers made war on the Cherokees and forced them from their homes. They burned 36 Cherokee towns and the people escaped into the mountains, leaving their crops and belongings behind. Nanye'hi, the Little Carpenter, and even Oconostota called for a lasting peace.

But Dragging Canoe would have none of it. He left the towns on the Little Tanasi River, and with his supporters went south to a place called Chickamauga Creek near Lookout Mountain and built new homes. The Chickamaugas, as they were called, swore never to surrender to the Americans, to fight to the death.

With this split, the Little Carpenter, Oconostota, and the other old chiefs made peace with the Americans, giving up more than five million acres of land in new treaties. This made Dragging Canoe madder than ever. He raided the place where the treaty was being signed, stealing the whites' horses and even killing a few men. Then he went north, killing and scalping the families of several settlers.

Nanye'hi felt helpless and rode to Chickamauga Creek to talk with her cousin. He sat silent before the fire as she spoke. His wife was busy shaving his head except for his scalp-lock worn long in the center, braided with feathers and beads. His face which might never again smile looked fierce with its pock-marks and scars of battle.

"My cousin, you must listen to reason. Fighting will not save us. Throw down your weapons. Come home with me. If you quit the fight, your warriors will give it up, too," she said.

He was unmoved by her talk. "You speak but I do not hear it," he said. "I am deaf to your words. You are no more to me than the wind blowing through the trees."

She left his home. Outside, his warriors were gathered around, waiting. She knew them by reputation, and she had watched some grow up. A few were friends of her own son, Five Killer. She saw warriors called Nickajack, Doublehead and Bench.

At a distance stood a warrior known as Bloody Fellow, who had started his own village near Chickamauga Creek. He was standing with Little Owl, Dragging Canoe's younger brother.

Nanye'hi went to them, looking intently at her young cousin. "Your father needs you. Come home with me," she said.

"My father is an old man and he thinks old men's thoughts," Little Owl said.

"You have no place here," she said.

"I am sorry, cousin. This is the only place I belong. I have made my choice."

She turned away, then stopped to look back. "I am sorry, too. I am so very sorry," she said.

When she returned to Chota, she sent Five Killer to take Mrs. Bean home to the settlements.

"I almost don't want to go. I'm afraid of what I'll find back there," Mrs. Bean said.

"You must go. Nothing good will happen here," Nanye'hi said.

She went back to her cabin, not wanting to see Lydia Bean leave Chota. Perhaps the white woman would return home and explain that not all the Ani-Yun Wiya were full of violent hatred like her cousins Dragging Canoe and Little Owl. But she couldn't bear to watch Mrs. Bean go.

Even with all the practice she was getting, Nanye'hi still wasn't very good at saying good-bye.

ELEVEN

Even in uncertain times, life must continue. Nanye'hi's daughter Elizabeth, called Betsy by nearly everyone, married the Virginia commissioner to the Cherokees, Joseph Martin. There was a big wedding ceremony at Chota. Nanye'hi's brother Long Fellow came with his family and many followers. The Little Carpenter and Oconostota, both looking old and frail, were there. Even Little Owl came up from the Chickamauga towns. But Dragging Canoe refused to honor the wedding, furious that Betsy married a white man, and an American, at that.

Betsy moved to Joseph Martin's big home on the Great Island of the Holston River. She lived like a white woman, and Nanye'hi thought that was fine as long as she kept the Ani-Yun Wiya in her heart. Her husband was an important man, a friend of the famous Patrick Henry, governor of Virginia.

Catherine, Nanye'hi's older daughter, also married a white man, a trader, and moved from Chota to his home. Five Killer took a Cherokee woman for a wife. Seeing the young ones start families of their own, even in this hard time, was good. But it made Nanye'hi feel old.

When she saw the old leaders, the Carpenter and Oconostota and Tassel, noticing how feeble they had become, it made her feel even older. One hot June day she was working in her corn field outside Chota when she grew quite dizzy and finally collapsed to the ground. Five Killer found her there and carried her to the shade of a big tulip poplar tree.

"Mother! What is the matter?" he asked.

For some time she could not answer. “I’m growing old,” she said, finally, gasping for breath.

“Nonsense,” Five Killer told her. “It was just the hot sun that did it. You need to work in the cool of the day.”

She went home, lying in the darkness of the cabin, not eating anything, feeling very sick. That evening Five Killer came to see her, with a sad look on his face.

“I am sorry to tell you this, mother, but the Little Carpenter is dead,” he said. “He died just today, in his bed.”

She was silent a long time. Then she asked, “What time did he die?”

“This afternoon.”

“About the time you found me in the field?”

“That is what I am told,” Five Killer said.

The Little Carpenter’s funeral was a sad affair. One of the great men of the Ani-Yun Wiya lay dead, never to be replaced. His own son, Dragging

Canoe, was in a far-off place fighting the whites. He had been a man of peace, a voice the Real People needed now more than ever. Now he was gone.

Next to her stood Oconostota. He put a hand on her shoulder and began to cry. She held him close, as she would a child, amazed at how thin he was, how fragile he felt. This had been the Great Warrior, the Brave Man, the war leader. He would fight no more, she realized.

But the fight went on without him. Dragging Canoe ranged far to attack settlers and forts, then fell back to the safety of his remote Chickamauga towns. The Americans seemed unable to understand some of the Cherokees were peaceful, even while the Chickamaugas raged. They attacked Cherokee towns, killing and scalping every warrior they could find, often even killing women, as well. The Americans sold the prisoners they took in battle as slaves, sending them to work on plantations far away from home.

Nanye'hi was shocked at the bitterness and hatred. There was no reason for any of it. The Cherokees gave up more land to the whites in new treaties. The very mountains seemed to be closing down around them. Still, it wasn't enough.

An American captain, James Robertson, came to live at Chota, watching the movements of the Cherokees, making sure the English had no claim on them. He did what he could to further divide the Cherokees near Chota from those at the Chickamauga towns. While the Chickamauga warriors were out raiding, Robertson's force of whites destroyed their hidden towns, burning much corn and capturing horses and cattle and English-made weapons.

When Robertson came back to Chota, Nanye'hi went to talk with him. "You live among us but you must hate us," she said.

"This is a war, Nancy," he said. "We Americans are fighting for our freedom. The Cherokees side with the English. We have no choice but to defend ourselves. You must bring in your warriors to talk peace. As long as Dragging Canoe is out there killing Americans, there can be no peace."

"You ask me to do something that I cannot do," she said. "Dragging Canoe has no ears for me. But I tell you this. You must leave Chota. The young men here would like to see your blood stain the ground. You kill their brothers and cousins, even their sisters. You must go."

And so Robertson did go. But the war continued, as the fighting increased between the Americans and the English all across the nation. To Nanye'hi's sorrow, even the men of Chota rode against the Americans. Even Five Killer took up weapons, striking deep into the settlements with his uncle Long Fellow.

In December 1780, a large force of whites under Colonel William Campbell marched down the river against the Cherokee towns. As they turned for

Chota, Nanye'hi went to speak to Campbell. She saw Betsy's husband Joseph Martin, now an army major, with the troops. But first she went to Campbell.

"You must spare us," she said. "We mean you no harm."

"Then why do your men try to kill us?" the colonel asked.

"They are afraid. And they fight to protect their homes and families. They do not understand this war between brothers, between the Americans and the English."

"We have had many treaties and still there is no peace," the colonel said.

"Many treaties and much of the Cherokee land is lost forever. We only want to live alone, in peace. I ask you now, as the Ghigau of my people, to put down your guns and fight no more."

"I am sorry, Nancy," he said. "I cannot do that. But if you want to be our friend, you can help us.

We have been on the march a long time and my men are starving. We are living on roots and berries. Can you bring us food? Can you show mercy to us?"

She looked in his eyes and saw a man in pain. "I will see what I can do," she said.

She went home and had some young men drive a herd of cows to the soldiers, so they might have something to eat.

But on December 28, less than two weeks later, the troops burned Chota and the neighboring towns of Tellico and Little Tuskegee. The soldiers went through the Cherokees' possessions and in Oconostota's cabin found papers sent to him by the English soldiers. They proved he fought against the Americans, Campbell said, and that all the Cherokees were treacherous.

Most of the Cherokees ran into the forest to escape the attack. Nanye'hi refused to run, though. The soldiers captured her, Five Killer and his family. Nanye'hi and her family went peacefully, not arguing or fighting.

She spoke again to Colonel Campbell, not fearing him or even hating him. He was nervous, not wanting to look her in the eye, ashamed of what he had done.

After a few days, he let her go and she took her family with her. They went home and stood looking at the ruins of Chota. She poked about in her charred burned-out cabin, and sighed deeply, thinking of all the bad things that had happened during her life. She looked upward and saw a hawk streak across the sky.

Turning to Five Killer, she said, "Come, we have much work to do."

They set about rebuilding Chota, the destroyed capital town of the Real People.

TWELVE

Nanye'hi was born to people of the Wolf Clan, the Aniwaya. In both war and peace they stood first for the Ani-Yun Wiya. Now the real wolves of the forest were becoming hard to find, killed by hunters or run off by the settlers. And Nanye'hi's own people were fewer and fewer, destroyed by the whites, by war and disease.

The Wolf Clan was great and mighty in the history of the Ani-Yun Wiya, she thought. And then she began to chant, "Tsun waya-ya, wa-a; Tsun waya-ya, wa-a; . . . I become a real wolf; I become a real wolf."

It was a chant from her childhood, one she had heard the elders make in ceremonies that were both secret and sacred. "I become a real wolf," she chanted. "Tsun waya-ya, wa-a . . . "

She crouched upon the ground and pawed like a wolf might do, scratching dirt with her hands, feeling the power of the wild wolf run deep within her body.

The old people said that at the creation, the wolf lived in the villages and the dog in the mountains. During the winter, the dog was cold and came down to the villages and drove the wolf to the mountains, taking its place by the fire. In the wild, the wolf became fierce and returned to the villages and killed some dogs. The people followed the wolf to the mountains and killed him but other wolves attacked the people with such fierceness that the people feared them and ever after would not hurt the wolves.

They believed it took a man with special powers to hunt wolves. An ordinary man could not do it.

Now, though, the rifle and its bullets and hunger drove the wolves from the mountains.

"Tsun waya-ya, wa-a," she chanted. "I become a real wolf. Tsun waya-ya, wa-a."

And she felt she was one. She felt the purity of the wolf within her body.

She was a wolf.

THIRTEEN

By the days of hot weather in 1781, the Cherokees were tired of war. Except for Dragging Canoe's Chickamaugas, who were also hurt by the white strikes forcing them to move their towns, the Real People arranged for a treaty on the Great Island of the Holston.

Nanye'hi went to the treaty-making with Oconostota, his son Terrapin, who was beginning to take his place at the council, and many other leaders of the Ani-Yun Wiya. She thought the white soldiers, with their weapons and fine clothes, looked pitiful and out of place along the wild river. Then she realized this was more and more their place, and less that of her people.

Her daughter Betsy was there, happy to see her

mother, and she had a child, a son, Nanye'hi had never seen before. The baby looked like a white child and Nanye'hi thought that might be best, since the child would live in a white world.

The men of the treaty council were surprised when Nanye'hi left the women's group and asked to speak to the men. No woman had ever spoken at a treaty-making. Then Colonel John Sevier, an important man who had been one of the soldiers who ate the cattle Nanye'hi had driven to feed the troops as they marched on Chota the winter before, waved her in.

She looked around at the commissioners, every one silent and watching her. Without pausing, she said, "You know that women are always looked upon as nothing. But we are your mothers. You are our sons. Our cry is all for peace. Let it continue. This peace must last forever. Let your women's sons be ours, our sons be yours. Let your women hear our words."

It was all she could think to say, but it was enough. Among the whites, Colonel William Christian rose to reply. He spoke to Nanye'hi and faced the group of women sitting nearby. He said, "Mothers, we have listened well to your talk. It is humane. No man can hear it without being moved by it. Such words and thoughts show the world that human nature is the same everywhere. Our women shall hear your words, and we know how they will feel and think of them. We are all descendants of the same woman. We will not quarrel with you, because you are our mothers. We will not meddle with your people if they will be still and quiet at home and let us live in peace."

After the treaty had been signed, the white men pushed around Nanye'hi, wanted to meet her, to touch this woman they'd heard so much about. She heard them talking about her. "That's Nancy Ward," they would say to each other. "Nancy Ward, Nancy Ward . . ."

She stood tall, looking most of the men in the eye, telling them to go home, to put their guns away and tend to their families. These were the men who had burned Chota and the other villages. These men thought it fun to kill Cherokee women and babies if the warriors weren't around to make a fight of it.

But she showed no fear. She pitied their greed and ignorance. She went home, not expecting a lasting peace because it seemed that wasn't in the hearts of men.

That summer, the corn crop was good. She tended it, picking the insects from it, pulling grass from the field. The Corn Spirit was that of a woman, the Ani-Yun Wiya believed. The plant sprang from a woman's blood and that is why it was called Agawela, The Old Woman.

Once a hunter had no luck but dreamed of a beautiful woman's singing throughout the night. The next day he found the singing coming from a stalk of corn growing in the forest. The corn stalk taught him the secrets of hunting, talking and singing through the morning until the sun rose high in the sky.

Then the corn plant changed into the form of a woman and disappeared into the air. Back home, after the hunter told his story, the elders decided the beautiful woman who grew from the corn stalk had been Selu, wife of Kanati, the Lucky Hunter.

The Ani-Yun Wiya needed Selu to come back, to give them some more luck, Nanye'hi thought. Even after the peace treaty had been signed, many warriors were killed and many women and children went hungry. Dragging Canoe's Chickamaugas now raided north, south, and west, and many women among his followers were widows, coming home to their families on the towns of the Little Tanasi with tales of horror.

John Sevier led raiders against Dragging Canoe, punishing him, taking women and children prisoner, but still the great warrior would not give up.

By the end of 1781, Oconostota said he would not live long. He could hardly see and it was painful for him to walk. He and Nanye'hi went with her daughter Betsy and Joseph Martin to their home on the Holston River, to spend his last winter in peace and quiet. The old warrior spoke of his past glory, the history of his people. He said he always wanted peace, even when the white people moved across the mountains to the land of the Cherokee.

When spring came, Oconostota was still alive. But he wanted to die in Chota. Jospeh Martin and some other men took Nanye'hi and Oconostota home in canoes. He died almost as soon as the canoes touched the bank near the Chota. Before he breathed his last breath, though, he asked to be buried as white people were, and to face his body toward the Long Knife, or the white people.

They made a casket from one of the canoes, dug

a grave, and placed Oconostota to face the white settlements. Joseph Martin read from his bible and prayed over the grave as Nanye'hi looked through the surrounding forest for Oconostota's spirit hovering among the trees.

First the Little Carpenter died. Now Oconostota. The Great Warrior of the Real People was gone.

All he'd wanted was peace. But he never found it. Neither did the Real People. The fighting continued, even after the English and the Americans signed their treaty in late 1782 saying the Americans won the war and now possessed all the land.

In the autumn of 1785 there was yet another peace treaty between the Americans and the Ani-Yun Wiya. This time the commissioners met at Hopewell, South Carolina. Nanye'hi rode there, again asking to speak to the group.

She went around the circle of commissioners, talking to them, shaking hands with some, and then spoke. "I hope that you have taken us by the hand in friendship," she said. "We hope the chain of friendship will never more be broken. I have a pipe and a little tobacco to give to the commissioners to smoke in friendship. I have seen much trouble in the late war. I am now old, but hope yet to bear children who will grow up and people our nation, as we are now under the protection of Congress and have no more disturbances. The talk that I give you is from myself."

Put down the weapons, live the words of brotherhood on the paper, and peace would come. But even as she said the words, she knew it was not likely.

FOURTEEN

The first child who came to her in her old age was a young boy, half-white just as she was half-white, rejected and despised by the Real People. He was an outcast. She took him in and called him Suyeta, "The Chosen One."

On their long walks through the fields and forests, he at first had little to say. Then a girl came to them. She was also half-white and alone in the world. Nanye'hi called her Astai'yi, "Strong Girl," because she was tough, surviving when a weak child would have died.

Suyeta and Astai'yi lived as brother and sister. They began to talk to each other, and to Nanye'hi, walking together, and told their stories of growing up in a time of war. Soon other children came to stay with Nanye'hi, filling her big cabin with laughter.

Most of them were strangers when they came to Chota. But word got around among the Real People that the Ghigau would take in those who needed help. Women began to come to Nanye'hi, too. They were widows or wives of warriors who nursed their defeat by drinking the white man's liquor. Too often they came marked and scarred by the violence of their husbands.

Nanye'hi put them all to work in the fields, growing food, and cooking to feed the old and poor people among them.

The fighting soon was worse than ever. Colonel John Sevier's troops attacked the nearby town of Hiwassee and then up to Chilhowee Town. The headman there, Old Tassel, and his leaders Hanging Maw, Abram, and Abram's son came out to talk under a white flag of truce. But the whites took them captive, anyway, and executed them all.

After this, the Ani-Yun Wiya council voted to move the capital from Chota, the city of refuge, to Ustanali, far to the south in Georgia, well away from the white settlements. Most of the young men who could carry weapons joined Dragging Canoe's Chickamaugans to fight the whites.

Settlers began moving closer and closer to Chota, finally building homes directly across the river. The white children began bullying the young Cherokees. One day Suyeta came home with a knife wound in his arm. Nanye'hi began packing her things that afternoon, and they soon left, moving south toward the Ocoee River, where her brother Long Fellow still lived.

Nanye'hi had lived her life in this place. She knew every tree, every rock, every ripple in the river that ran past Chota. She loved it with a love that was deeper than any other love she had ever felt. Yet, now she was leaving it, with her life's belongings packed onto three mule-drawn wagons, her herd of cattle drifting along behind, tended by four small boys.

But the Chota that she saw now was not the Chota she had known. Now there were only a few people in it, most of the cooking fires put out. Once the decisions that had led the nation were made here, and she had been a part of them. The Carpenter and Oconostota had walked this ground. Her friend Blossom lived and died here, grieving for three husbands killed in battle. Her children were born here.

All gone. Chota was past, no more than grass that fades with the first chill of autumn, or the leaves that drift from the trees. For her, Chota was gone.

She turned her face toward the Ocoee River and the Amovey District, where many of her family had gone seeking a peaceful place to live. Long Fellow was glad to see her. He made room for the orphans and widows traveling with her, fixing small cabins around his property for them. Nanye'hi stayed for a while with Catherine, telling her grandchildren Nannie and Elizabeth the old stories.

She would start out, "I once heard the old ones say," and the girls would quiet and listen as she told them the tale of the Ice Man, the Great Leech, the Slant-Eyed Giant, the Man who married Thunder's Sister, and the other old stories of the Ani-Yun Wiya.

These girls, even with all their white blood, needed to know the stories of their people. And even though Nannie and Elizabeth's father was white, that didn't matter, Nanye'hi knew. For the Ani-Yun Wiya, the true blood, clan relationships, ran through the women. These girls would always be of the Real People.

Back at Long Fellow's town, she helped farm but that wasn't enough. She organized a dance where the men dancing dropped goods on blankets which were then given to the poor. It was a hard time for many people. They were hungry, dressed in rags. The young men who could have hunted were off fighting with Dragging Canoe.

Finally, she sat with her brother, talking about what she could do with her life. "I cannot just sit and bide my time," she said.

"You are the Ghigau. You need do nothing," Long Fellow said.

"I am the Ghigau, and that means I must do something with my life. I cannot wait for death to take me," she said.

"You are a wealthy woman. You have saved every penny you ever made. And look at all these people who depend on you. You can do anything you want. Never in the history of the Ani-Yun Wiya has there been a woman like you. No woman has ever had your power, the power to speak her mind to anyone who would listen. No woman has done the things you have done, Beloved Woman."

She stood, looking out the door of his house at the Milky Way sweeping far overhead in the night sky. "Tomorrow I will go find something," she said. "I was pushed out of Chota but somewhere there is a place for me."

FIFTEEN

In 1792, Dragging Canoe died. He and his followers had been celebrating all night after taking some white scalps. The next day he tried to rise, reached for his heart, and fell back, dead. Old Tassel's nephew, John Watts, also called Young Tassel, took his place as the war leader.

Bloody Fellow and a group of his friends went to Philadelphia to meet with the American president, George Washington. The president agreed to give the Cherokees $1,500 each year in payment for their lands, and gave Bloody Fellow a new name, Iskagua, meaning "Clear Sky." He took an American flag home with him, flying it over his home at the foot of Lookout Mountain.

Within a year, though, Doublehead, his brother Pumpkin Boy and their nephew Bench, were raiding American settlers all the way up into Kentucky. Even so, in 1794, Doublehead went back to Philadelphia, arranging to get $5,000 in trade goods each year for the Cherokees. He and his followers kept the goods for themselves, and the poor Cherokees in the Overhill towns got nothing.

Later that year, the Americans destroyed the towns of the Chickamaugans, striking deep into their country. By autumn, they were ready for peace. Bloody Fellow, John Watts, the Glass, Pathkiller, Stallion, and forty chiefs signed the treaty paper at Tellico Blockhouse.

The Cherokees took up the plow, learning again to farm the land. Nanye'hi, knowing how plants grew, helped them get started. She traveled from town to town, explaining how to make corn grow to all the young men and women of the Ani-Yun Wiya who had known nothing but war. They had lost the old skills, and she spent her days teaching.

She showed them how to milk cows and make cheese and butter, the things Lydia Bean had taught her long ago. She explained the best ways of feeding the cattle, and of helping the young calves live and grow.

Back at the Ocoee, she rented land from her son-in-law and fenced in five acres of corn so the roaming hogs and wild animals could not get it. She planted two acres of cotton, a half-acre of potatoes and another half-acre of peanuts. She began raising chickens, both for the meat and the eggs.

Suyeta and Astai'yi were still with her. She put them to work in the fields, and the crops grew tall and thick.

As in the old days, they held a Green Corn Dance. Everyone came for the ball-play, the speeches, the feasts, and, of course, the dancing.

After Nanye'hi sold some of her crops, she went

to the Woman Killer Ford on the Ocoee River and bought an inn. Travelers could stay there, but she mostly was looking for a large house that could hold all the orphan children and widows that still came to live with her. Suyeta and Astai'yi were old enough to help organize work crews for cleaning the house, planting the fields, and caring for the animals.

More and more people came to stay, wanting to be near the Beloved Woman of the Ani-Yun Wiya. Some had money. Some were poor. She took them all in.

"Grandmother, there is no room for everyone," Suyeta said one day. "We have to turn some away."

"Never," Nanye'hi said. "These are my people and my home is always open to them."

The inn became known as Granny Ford. For Nanye'hi, it was a little Chota, a place of refuge, where people with troubles could come and rest in peace. And she didn't care whether the people were Cherokee or white or even Creek.

"The same sky covers us all," she said.

It seemed strange to be called Granny. She still felt like the young woman who had gone with Kingfisher to the battle of Taliwa against the Creeks many years before. In her mind, she was young and strong.

Yet, the mirror told her she was becoming gray-haired now. Her skin was still smooth and her back was straight but it was true she was growing old, just as the Carpenter had grown old, just as Oconostota and Tame Doe had.

Knowing the years were catching up with her made her work harder, however. "I have much to do," she told Long Fellow one day when he visited. "Much to do and little time left."

SIXTEEN

Somewhere in the seven heavens there is a place for the Ani-Yun Wiya, Nanye'hi thought. In one of the seven directions, the wind must blow warm upon the Real People. Under one of the seven sacred trees, there is a shade to cover them.

"We must have our place," she told her son Five Killer, who was visiting at the inn. "The Ani-Yun Wiya cannot be scattered across the earth with no home."

The tribal council was meeting at Amovey but Nanye'hi was too feeble to go. The women's council had come and talked with her about the meeting, which was to discuss selling more land to the whites and, possibly, even moving to the country across the Mississippi River far to the west. Her granddaughters Jenny McIntosh, Caty Harlan and Elizabeth Walker were there, with nine other women. Everyone agreed the Ani-Yun Wiya had given up enough land already, and to move would be a great hardship.

Nanye'hi asked Jenny to write her words in a letter to the council. She spoke softly, her face dark and thoughtful. "Our beloved children and head-men of the Cherokee nation, we address you warriors in council. We have raised all of you on the land which we now have, which God gave us to inhabit and raise provisions. We know that our country has once been extensive but by repeated sales has become circumscribed to a small tract and never have thought it our duty to interfere in the disposition of it till now," she said, pausing for Jenny to write it all down.

" . . . Your mothers, your sisters ask and beg of you not to part with any more of our lands. We say

. . . keep it for our growing children for it was the good will of our creator to place us here. And you know our father the great president will not allow his white children to take our country away. Only keep your hands off of paper talks. For it is our own country . . .

"Therefore, children, don't part with any more of our lands but continue on it and enlarge your farms and cultivate and raise corn and cotton and we your mothers and sisters will make clothing for you . . .

" . . . Nancy Ward to her children. Warriors take pity and listen to the talks of your sisters. Although I am very old, I yet cannot but pity the situation in which you will hear of their minds. I have a great many grandchildren which I wish them to do well on our land."

Nanye'hi signed her name, "Nancy Ward" in big letters at the bottom of the paper. The other women signed after her.

Now she gave the paper to Five Killer to take to the tribal council meeting. "I want you to take my walking stick," she said, holding the gnarled piece of wood out for her son. "It is my symbol. With this stick, I am at the council meeting."

The warriors listened, but it made no difference. They were confused, living more and more like the whites, yet still in conflict with them. The whites wanted land. More and more of the Cherokees did not know exactly what they wanted.

Nanye'hi was greatly disturbed. Another treaty was signed, the Hiwassee Treaty of 1819. It gave all the Little Tanasi River valley to the whites. Even though Nanye'hi had not lived there for years, even though Chota was empty, it was a painful thing to know the old homeplace was forever out of the hands of her people.

"You know how I got my name, do you not?" she asked her little great-grandson Jack Hildebrand one day.

"Nancy Ward?" the boy asked.

"No, people now call me that, or Granny. But my name is Nanye'hi. It comes from the story of the Nunne'hi, the spirit people who live forever. It means 'people who live anywhere' or maybe 'one who goes about.' "

"Where are the spirit people?" Jack asked.

"They live under the mountains, under the Land of Blue Smoke," she said. "They can make themselves invisible, or they can look like real people. They spend their time singing and dancing. You can hear them on the wind at night. That sound you hear in the mountains, that's the Nunne'hi."

Nanye'hi stopped to light her pipe. Puffing, she continued the story. "They are great warriors, too, and come out to help the Ani-Yun Wiya when they need them most. They have saved us from defeat many times. The Nunne'hi women are very beautiful and the young men fall in love with them when they visit the dances in the towns. When the young men follow them into the mountains, the Nunne'hi women disappear into the ground."

"Can the Nunne'hi help us now?" Jack asked.

Nanye'hi looked at him, puffing the pipe. Little Jack's mother, Nanye'hi's granddaughter Elizabeth was just a little older than Nanye'hi had been at the battle of Taliwa when Kingfisher was killed and Nanye'hi had been named the Ghigau. Elizabeth looked like a white woman but she and little Jack both needed to know the ways of the Ani-Yun Wiya.

"I think now the Nunne'hi are gone. It's going to take the power of a little fellow like you to bring them back," Nanye'hi said. "I was named after them and I think I am the closest thing left to a Nunne'hi. I will do my best, but I cannot work their magic."

Nanye'hi began to feel very old in the days to come. She stayed in the inn as long as she could. Then she asked to be moved to her brother Long

Fellow's home not far away. There, she would be closer to her grandchildren.

She liked to sit on the porch, talking of her childhood, telling the tales of the Ani-Yun Wiya. She wanted the children to always remember the greatness of the Real People.

One day she was very sick and asked for all her grandchildren and great-grandchildren who were in the area to come to see her. They crowded into the room on a warm spring day in 1822. She was quiet and seemed very small lying in her big bed. She talked to each of the children, telling them some little thing they could remember as they grew.

Finally, she sat up a little, looking at everyone gathered before her. "It is no terrible thing to grow old," she said. "It is no terrible thing to die. It is only terrible to fear it. And I don't."

She lay back down, calling Five Killer. He brought her swan wing fan, putting it in her hands crossed on her chest. "I am still the Ghigau," she said, smiling.

And then she died. Those in the room saw a light rise from her body, circling the bed several times, pausing up near the ceiling. Then it went out the door, fluttering like a bird, like a white swan, like the spirit of the Ghigau.

Once outside, the light went north, over the rolling hills, speeding past the pines and poplars and oaks, beyond the new settlements, toward the city of refuge, toward Chota, the place that now existed only in the hearts of those who had lived in it.

The Ghigau had gone home.

EPILOGUE

Nanye'hi, the Ghigau, Nancy Ward, was buried on a hillside not far from the Woman Killer Ford of the Ocoee River. The town of Benton, Tennessee later grew up nearby. Her brother Long Fellow and son Five Killer were buried in the same plot. The graves went unmarked for a century. In 1923, the Nancy Ward Chapter of the Daughters of the American Revolution placed a stone marker on her grave, with a bronze tablet honoring her life.

The Cherokees were unable to fight the greed of the white settlers. A gold rush in Georgia led to all the Cherokees forfeiting their land, including the 640 acres Nancy Ward gave before her death to her granddaughter Jenny McIntosh.

Except for a small remnant that hid in the North

Carolina mountains, the Cherokees were forced to move from their homeland to the Oklahoma Territory by 1838. Most of the old Cherokee capital of Chota has been underwater since the Tennessee Valley Authority dammed the Little Tennessee River in 1979. The site of the Council House remains on dry land about 12 miles from Vonore, Tennessee, however. Alongside the water, markers from each of the Cherokee clans show where Nancy Ward, the Carpenter and Oconostota worked for their people.

Nanye'hi was the last true Ghigau of the Ani-Yun Wiya living in the valleys of the Land of Blue Smoke. Maggie Wachacha, a member of the Snowbird Cherokees in Graham County, N.C., was given the ceremonial title of Beloved Woman late in life for her long years of service to her people. She died in February 1993 at the age of 98.

After Nanye'hi, no one ever again performed the

duties of the Ghigau. Her dream of peace went unfulfilled. Her people lost their land. But she left a legacy of strength and pride and truth to inspire people of all races and nations.

Call her name: Nanye'hi, Spirit Woman, Nancy Ward, Wild Rose, Beloved Woman. The Cherokees never had another.

About the Author

Charles Blake Johnson is Southern editor of *Farm Journal* magazine. His other books include *Bailout,* an adventure novel. He lives in the Smoky Mountains of Tennessee, the Cherokees' Land of Blue Smoke, not far from the place where Nancy Ward worked for peace among her people.